On 23rd December, Santa and the Elves were busy, making final preparations for Christmas Eve's present delivery.

Mrs. Claus was cooking a meal fit for kings and queens,
with baskets of carrots, hay and reindeer greens.

While delivering hay and carrots to the reindeer's table,
Mrs. Claus discovered that Rudolf was missing from his stable.

All of the Elves looked high and low,
But where Rudolf was they did not know.

Sadly Rudolf was absent without leave,
But for Santa it was take-off time, it was now Christmas Eve.

While the Elves were getting ready to deliver presents,
Rudolf was discovering the Cayman Islands and its sandy crescents.

Rudolf had flown from the North Pole and landed on the Bluff in Cayman Brac.
He explored the island from the North East Point Lighthouse to Rebecca's Cave, to West End and back.

Rudolf then flew to Little Cayman and was amazed at the beauty of the place.
He saw the Bloody Bay diving wall and wished he could scuba dive in that deep blue space.

East End, Grand Cayman was next on Rudolf's list.
He loved the Blow Holes, viewed through the salty mist.

On then to North Side, Rum Point and the Mastic Trail.
Followed by the Sandbar to see the stingrays and their stinging tails.

Next Rudolf visited Pedro St. James Castle, William Eden's plantation home,
A most interesting landmark, but Rudolf had further to roam.

Rudolf continued his exploration down South Sound,
and over George Town's Hog Sty Bay where the tourists walk around.

On to the Head of Barkers, thinking of all the girls and boys,
Rudolf knew that he should be out delivering their gifts and toys.

Meanwhile over Jamaica, at a very great height,
Santa was bedazzled by a bright red light.
It seemed to come from Cayman, in the distance to the West
could it be Rudolf, as Blitzen had guessed?

Rudolf sobbed, "The Reindeer were calling me names so I left the North Pole. I flew on the Christmas winds, landing in the Brac, on the Bluff's large knoll."

Rudolf and the Reindeer were reunited,
And when asked to guide the sleigh Rudolf was delighted.

The Reindeer were sorry for calling Rudolf names,
And how happy to have Rudolf back they proclaimed.

Rudolf said "Santa, the Cayman Islands are amazing
with so many good boys and girls the parents are proudly raising."

Santa said "I visit the Cayman Islands every year on my sleigh, delivering toys with which children play."

They delivered gifts to George Town and Seven Mile Beach.
As far as West Bay they did reach.

On to Bodden Town, the Island's first capital, the Reindeer flew.
Next, the children of East End received their gifts too.

Finally the sleigh reached the children of North Side
The sleigh was then emptied, noted Santa with pride.

Congratulating Rudolf for a job well done,
Santa invited him for a week's holiday in the sun.

The moral of the story, if you really want to know,
with good old Rudolf reindeer flying high and flying low,
taking parcels round at Christmas, or helping out at home,
it's good to think of others, wherever we might roam.